N.B. N.B. N.B. N.B. N.B. N.B.

It has been suggested ~~by another reader that~~
~~this book is controversial because~~ that

Rupert books are controversial
because they portray
stereotypical character

Please exercise discretion if using this book in
school.

RUPERT

AND THE DRAGON SWEETS

Written by
MIKE TRUMBLE

Based on a story by Alfred Bestall MBE

BBC BOOKS

Published by BBC Books,
A division of BBC Enterprises Ltd
Woodlands, 80 Wood Lane, London W12 0TT

First published 1989

Rupert Bear and Characters
© Express Newspapers Plc 1989

Text © Michael Trumble and
Express Newspapers Plc 1989
ISBN 0 563 20746 9 (Hardback)
ISBN 0 563 20745 0 (Paperback)

Typeset in Plantin 12/14 pt.
by Keyspools Ltd, Warrington

Colour separations by Dot Gradations Ltd, Chelmsford
Printed in Great Britain by Cambus Litho, East Kilbride
Cover printed by Fletchers of Norwich

Magic
Adventur e P

Pong Ping has invited Rupert to his home
To see his baby pet dragon.
"Why not stroke him?" says the little pekinese,
"He won't bite you, go on."

The little bear's not so sure, and as he strokes
The fierce-looking animal,
It roars and puffs out fire. "Oh dear," he says,
"Your pet doesn't like me at all!"

"Don't be alarmed, my friend," cries Pong Ping,
Taking a jar from a drawer,
"Give him one of these magic Dragon Sweets,
Then he'll be calm and won't roar."

The little peke smiles as he watches Rupert
Give his pet a Dragon Sweet.
"You see," he says as they go into the garden,
"He's quiet now, it's worked a treat.

Dragons would do anything for a Dragon Sweet,
They really love them," says Pong Ping.
"They only need to eat just one of them
And they're always very loving."

"What's up with your pet?" cries Rupert suddenly.
"Something's given it a fright!"
But as the chums run to see what's upset it,
The baby dragon takes flight.

"Now I'll never get him back!" cries Pong Ping,
"Oh dear me, what shall I do?"
"You don't have to worry, Pong Ping," says Rupert,
"I know how to get him for you.

Quickly, give me some more of the Dragon Sweets,
I'm sure he'll come for those."
So Pong Ping gives him a handful of sweets
And off the little bear goes.

On Nutwood common Rupert spies fiery smoke
Coming from the top of a tree.
He runs over to it, knowing that's where
The baby dragon's sure to be.

Rupert takes his time and climbs the tree
Very carefully, in case he falls.
At the top sits Pong Ping's dragon,
"I've a sweet for you," he calls.

But the baby dragon doesn't want the sweet
And makes an awful crying sound,
Which hurts the little bear's ears so much
He has to climb to the ground.

As he walks away, a big dragon appears,
Flying very high in the sky.
"My goodness," cries Rupert, "it must have heard
That baby dragon's strange cry."

Seeing such a huge beast flying nearer
Gives Rupert a dreadful shock.
He runs away as fast as he can
And hides behind a large rock.

But the dragon sees him and roars loudly,
Breathing out fire as it flies down.
"I do hope the Dragon Sweets work on him,"
Says Rupert with a worried frown.

"Here, big dragon, I've a nice sweet for you,"
The little bear calls out bravely,
And it takes the sweet, gobbles it all up
And is soon very friendly.

Suddenly the baby dragon leaps onto its back,
As it stands there still and calm.
"This is my chance to catch him," thinks Rupert,
"I'm sure I won't come to any harm."

But the dragon spreads its wings as he climbs on,
And quickly takes to the air,
Carrying with him Pong Ping's baby dragon and
A very worried little bear.

Rupert holds tight with all of his strength,
To the back of the great beast
As it flies at speed over sea and land
To a castle in the Far East.

Both the dragons fly away, so Rupert
Goes up to the castle door.
A big stern guard answers it and marches him
Along a marble corridor.

Then he's led by two more men to a room
At the top of some stone stairs.
"This is Dragon Land," says an old man,
"It's no place for little bears!

"I'm the Emperor, tell me how you came.
And for what reason."
"I came here by accident," says Rupert,
"On the back of a big dragon."

"That's impossible," cries the Emperor,
"Your story just can't be true!
Nobody has ever ridden on a dragon,
So how on earth could you?"

Then Rupert tells him about the Dragon Sweets
And how he came to Dragon Land.
The Emperor listens and smiles broadly
As he begins to understand.

"I'm very worried about Pong Ping's pet,"
Says the worried little bear.
"He flew away as soon as we landed, but
I think he's still here somewhere."

"Well, it won't be difficult to find him,"
Says the kind old Emperor,
"All the baby dragons in Dragon Land
Will be summoned by my trumpeter."

The trumpet's blown and lots of baby dragons
Come to the very strange sound
And, because he's wearing a red collar,
Pong Ping's pet is quickly found.

"Thank you for finding him for me," says Rupert,
"But how can we get home from here?"
"I've thought about that," says the Emperor,
"Come with me, I have an idea.

That rocket has room for the baby dragon
And, of course, for you, little bear,
It'll take you both home in no time at all.
It goes very fast through the air."

So Rupert says goodbye to the Emperor and,
With Pong Ping's dragon pet,
He goes up some tall wooden step ladders
And climbs into the rocket.

Its big fuse is lit and, with a loud roar,
It rises into the sky.
Rupert sees Dragon Land disappear far below
As the rocket soars up high.

Suddenly the rocket's capsule breaks away,
And tumbles down through the sky.
To Rupert's relief, a big parachute opens,
"Thank goodness," he says with a sigh.

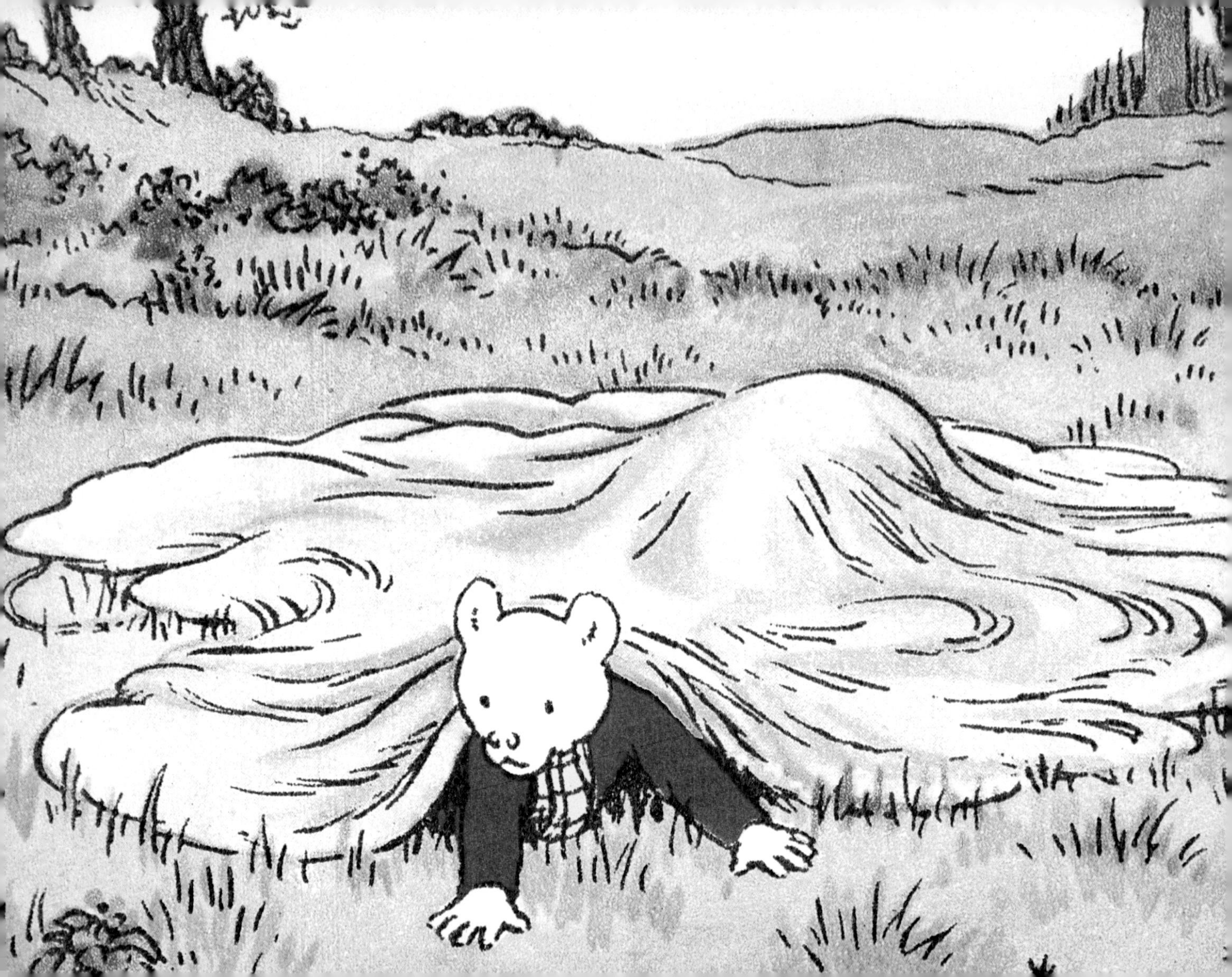

Quietly and gently the capsule floats down
And alights upon the ground,
Rupert crawls from beneath the parachute,
Very pleased he's safe and sound.

"Pong Ping," cries Rupert, as the peke arrives,
"I've got your pet dragon for you,
And had an adventure with the Dragon Sweets
That's hard to believe, but true."

The happy peke helps to uncover the capsule
Where his pet baby dragon sleeps,
"Thank you, Rupert, for bringing him home to me,"
He says, "You're my best friend for keeps."